William Augustus Muhlenberg

**I would not live always**

1st edition

William Augustus Muhlenberg

**I would not live always**
*1st edition*

ISBN/EAN: 9783743328686

Manufactured in Europe, USA, Canada, Australia, Japa

Cover: Foto ©Andreas Hilbeck / pixelio.de

Manufactured and distributed by brebook publishing software
(www.brebook.com)

William Augustus Muhlenberg

**I would not live always**

# I WOULD NOT LIVE ALWAY,

AND

Other Pieces in Verse by the same Author.

———

NEW YORK:

ROBERT CRAIGHEAD, PRINTER.

1860.

TO

# MY DEAR SISTER,

## The Treasurer of My Verses,

### THIS SELECTION OF THEM

## IS AFFECTIONATELY INSCRIBED.

W. A. M.

# PREFATORY NOTE.

I LITTLE thought that I should ever gather up my metres, to make a book of them. Besides other reasons, they are few in number. But I now do it, on the assurance that some profit may accrue in aid of the charity to which my life is at present devoted.

What *kind* of poetical merit these compositions possess I perfectly understand. Most of the Hymns are devotional lyrics rather than the earnest songs of Redemption. Would that they had the inspiration of Watts's or Wesley's lyre !

The first piece has appeared several times in print, but it is still so frequently asked for, and the Hymn which is a part of it has become so general a favorite, that perhaps it will give something of the expected value to the publication.

It was not thought worth while to reprint here, those Hymns of mine which are in the Prayer Book collection.

W. A. MUHLENBERG.

St. Luke's Hospital,
*December*, 1859.

# CONTENTS.

# I WOULD NOT LIVE ALWAY.

*Job* vii. 16.

I WOULD not live alway—live alway below !
Oh no, I'll not linger when bidden to go :
The days of our pilgrimage granted us here,
Are enough for life's woes, full enough for its cheer :
Would I shrink from the path which the prophets of
    God,
Apostles, and martyrs, so joyfully trod ?
Like a spirit unblest, o'er the earth would I roam,
While brethren and friends are all hastening home ?

I would not live alway : I ask not to stay,
Where storm after storm rises dark o'er the way;
Where seeking for rest we but hover around,
Like the patriarch's bird, and no resting is found;
Where Hope when she paints her gay bow in the air,
Leaves its brilliance to fade in the night of despair,
And joy's fleeting angel ne'er sheds a glad ray,
Save the gleam of the plumage that bears him away.

1*

I would not live alway—thus fettered by sin,
Temptation without and corruption within;
In a moment of strength if I sever the chain,
Scarce the victory is mine, ere I'm captive again ;
E'en the rapture of pardon is mingled with fears,
And the cup of thanksgiving with penitent tears :
The festival trump calls for jubilant songs,
But my spirit her own *miserere* prolongs.


I would not live alway—no, welcome the tomb,
Since Jesus hath lain there, I dread not its gloom;
Where He deigned to sleep, I'll too bow my head,
All peaceful to slumber on that hallowed bed.
Then the glorious day break, to follow that night,
The orient gleam of the angels of light,
With their clarion call for the sleepers to rise
And chant forth their matins, away to the skies.


Who, who would live alway ? away from his God,
Away from yon heaven, that blissful abode
Where the rivers of pleasure flow o'er the bright plains,
And the noon-tide of glory eternally reigns;
Where the saints of all ages, in harmony meet
Their Saviour and brethren, transported to greet,
While the songs of salvation exultingly roll,
And the smile of the Lord is the feast of the soul.

That heavenly musick ! hark, sweet in the air
The notes of the harpers how clear ringing there !
And see, soft unfolding those portals of gold,
The King all arrayed in His beauty behold !
Oh give me, Oh give me, the wings of a dove
To adore Him—be near Him—enrapt with His love ;
I but wait for the summons, I list for the word—
Alleluia—Amen—evermore with the Lord.

1824. Revised, 1859.

## "SINCE O'ER THY FOOTSTOOL."

Since o'er Thy footstool here below,
  Such radiant gems are strown,
Oh, what magnificence must glow,
  My God, about Thy throne!
So brilliant here these drops of light,
There the full ocean rolls, how bright!


If night's blue curtain of the sky,
  With thousand stars inwrought,
Hung like a royal canopy
  With glittering diamonds fraught,
Be, Lord, Thy temple's outer veil,
What splendor at the shrine must dwell!


The dazzling sun, at noontide hour,
  Forth from his flaming vase,
Flinging o'er earth the golden shower,
  Till vale and mountain blaze,
But shows, O Lord, one beam of Thine,
What, then, the day where Thou dost shine!

Ah! how shall these dim eyes endure
  That noon of living rays,
Or, how my spirit so impure
  Upon thy brightness gaze?
Anoint, O Lord, anoint my sight,
And robe me for that world of light.

1824.

# VESPER HYMN.

THE mellow eve is gliding,
  Serenely down the west,
So, every care subsiding,
  My soul would sink to rest.

The woodland hum is ringing
  The daylight's gentle close,
May dear ones round me singing,
  Thus hymn my last repose.

The evening star has lighted
  Her crystal lamp on high,
So when in death benighted,
  Let hope illume the sky.

In golden splendor burning,
  The morrow's dawn shall break;
Oh, on the last bright morning,
  May I in glory wake.

# ROSY JUNE.

Rosy June is descending,
   Her breath's in the air,
Light and beauty attending
   Her zephyr-drawn car :
Around her entwining
   Are rainbows of flowers,
Her coronal shining,
   With morn's dewy showers.

The woodbine is wreathing
   The lattice with bloom,
Magnolias are breathing
   Their spicy perfume,
The violets are flinging
   Their redolence sweet,
Blossoms everywhere springing,
   Her coming to greet.

The humming bird's sporting
   On gossamer wing,
The butterfly's courting
   Each beautiful thing,

The oriole is showing
　　His plumage of gold,
In gardens all glowing
　　Like Eden of old.

The blue waves are breaking
　　With mirth on the strand,
Wild music is waking
　　O'er river and land,
The moss-garnished fountains
　　All sparkling arise,
And forest-plumed mountains
　　Are kissing the skies.

Jocund breezes are blowing,
　　Joy flushes the scene,
In the tide health is flowing,
　　Life bounds in the green :
With mirth in all voices,
　　And hearts all in tune—
Glad nature rejoices
　　To hail Rosy June.

1826.

# TO THE EVENING STAR.

QUEEN of the twilight hour,
  I hail thy soothing reign ;
While silent 'neath thy power,
  Lie valley, hill, and plain.

How fair thy beauty glows
  Gem of the amber west !
Or, like a snowy rose
  Dew-bright on Evening's breast.

Nay, be a temple-light
  Lit for earth's vesper song,
On Heaven's high altar dight,
  The incense clouds among.

So by thy hallowed beams,
  From nature's book I'll pray,
And catch the bliss that seems
  Luxuriant in thy day.

# MUSICK.

Musick in voice, or pipe, or string,
  The dullest ear discerns ;
But to the soul's ear listening,
  Tuneful all nature turns.

Musick there is when morning springs
  On plumes of purple light ;
When evening softly folds her wings
  Upon the lap of night.

There's musick when the vernal gale
  Sings to the waking flowers ;
When sombre Autumn through the vale
  Her mellow anthem pours.

There's musick in the dancing light,
  Of moonbeams on the waves ;
Deep musick in the howling night,
  When the wild tempest raves.

There's musick in the sparkling stream
  That gems the mountain side ;
Rich musick in the golden gleam
  Of fields in harvest pride.

Grand musick in the starlight sky
   Ringing from out the spheres,
Those chords of nine-fold harmony
   Strung at the birth of years.

There's musick—say, where is there none?
   God's glorious works around,
Each gives in harmony its tone,
   A universe of sound.

# SUNDAY SCHOOL HYMN.

"Feed my Lambs."—*St. John* **xxi.** 15.

"Feed my Lambs," how condescending,
How compassionate the grace
Of the Saviour, just ascending,
Thus to bless our infant race.

Richest treasure, dearest token
From His stores of love to give,
Kept from age to age unbroken,
Till its bounty we receive.

Who, without that word of blessing
Could our dark estate have told?
Sin and woe our souls distressing,
Lost and wandering from His fold.

"Feed my Lambs," ye pastors hear it,
Feed the flock of His own hand;
Oh, for Him, for us revere it;
Keep the Shepherd's last command.

# "I'LL WORSHIP THE LORD."

"I will give thanks unto the Lord, with my whole heart, secretly among the faithful, and in the congregation."—*Psalm* lxi. 1.

I'll worship the Lord in His house,
    I'll haste with the church-going throng
At His altar to offer my vows,
    And join in the festival song.

I'll worship the Lord with the few
    Sojourners who meet by the way,
To muse of the Canaan in view,
    And for strength on their pilgrimage pray.

I'll worship the Lord in the ring,
    Where brothers and sisters unite
Every morning His goodness to sing,
    His mercy and truth every night.

But, oh, there's a temple besides,
    A temple, the world ne'er hath known,
Where ministering silence presides,
    And the heart is the altar alone.

To the High Priest Himself I'll draw near,
To His own mercy-seat in the Heaven,
Where the voice of His love meets mine ear:
" Go in peace—thy sins are forgiven."

# CRADLE SONG.

SWEET, my darling, be thy sleeping
　　Pillowed on affection's breast;
Love, her faithful watch is keeping,
　　Bending o'er thy smiling rest:
Thus nor care nor sorrow knowing
　　Be thy life a happy dream,
Ne'er through wild or desert flowing,
　　All thy days a gentle stream.

How adorned in opening beauty
　　Thou wilt grace thy parents' side!
Care of thee their fondest duty,
　　Thou alone their joy and pride.
Yes, my Lily, thou shalt flower
　　Like some plant of paradise;
Blight nor mildew touch thy bower,
　　Always bright thy genial skies.

Hush! my tongue, that idle singing
　　As if earth were fairy land;
Not below the joys are springing,
　　Not the bliss I would command.

Rather this thy mother's blessing,
This my daughter be thy share :
Graces of the soul possessing,
Be in virtue's mirror fair.

To the flock of Christ elected,
Oh, but know the Shepherd's love,
By His rod and staff protected
Onward to His fold above :
Be thy path then rough or even,
Few or many be thy days,
Only, so we meet in Heaven
Joining there in endless praise.

1828.

# HYMN FOR ADVENT.

" Then shall He sit upon the throne of his glory."

THE Throne of His Glory—as snow it is white,
Upborne in the air by the legions of Light,
And startled to life by the trumpet's last sound,
The hosts of the nations stand waiting around.

The Throne of His Glory—there lieth unsealed
The life-roll, the death-roll, of names ne'er revealed,
Now secret no longer : the millions divide
To the right and the left, on the throne's either side.

The Throne of His Glory—and glorious there stand
The elect of His love, and the sheep of His hand,
While, dark on His left, shrunk away from His face,
The lost ones that sought not the Throne of His Grace.

The Throne of His Glory—my poor trembling soul !
Oh, what, when arraigned there, thy dread shall
    control
Of that doom of the exiled, " Ye cursed depart,"
For ever, and ever, to toll on the heart.

2

From thy Father an exile? Thy home never see?
No, child of His mercy, unchanging and free,
Ere creation began, in the counsels of love,
He wrote thee an heir of His kingdom above.

1839.

# NEW YEAR'S EVE.

HARK! tis twelve o'clock tolling;
 The jovial cup,
As fast as time's rolling,
 With pleasure fill up:
Adieu pain and sorrow!
 Thou old year begone!
One long and bright morrow,
 Fair new year come on!

Hush, wild one, that laughter—
 That madness have done—
The past and hereafter,
 Believe it are one:
There needs not a seer
 To paint coming days,
Who scans the old year,
 On the new one may gaze.

Eyes that with pleasure
 Full brilliantly beam,
With grief's bitter treasure
 How surely ye'll stream;

Ears that are thrilling
   With rapturous song,
Cruel words shall be filling
   And anguish, ere long.

The dance, the regaling,
   The music, the feast;
Ah, weeping and wailing
   For where is the guest?
The light heart rebounding
   And leaping with mirth—
The white shroud surrounding,
   "Dust to dust—earth to earth."

Hark! the last bell is tolling,
   It tolls for the dead ;
Ere another year's rolling,
   What souls shall have fled !
Hush, wild one, that laughter,
   Look back on the past;
Lest, boasting hearafter,
   This year be thy last.
1830.

# HYMN FOR THE EPIPHANY.

*Isaiah* lx.

RISE, daughter of Zion, thy mourning is o'er,
The night that hath veiled thee shall veil thee no more;
Wear the robes of the morning, arise thou and shine,
For the beauty and light of Jehovah are thine.

Oh, lift up thine eyes, look around thee and see
How thy children are gathering together to thee;
Like doves on the wing, flying home to be blest
At thine altar with peace, in thy bosom with rest.

From the sea's furthest shores, and like its full tide,
The nations new-born, how they flow to thy side;
To freedom forth springing, thy light having seen,
They own thee a Mother, and hail thee a Queen.

Who wasted thee once, humbly kneel at thy feet,
Rejoicing thy sceptre of mercy to meet,
While the proud ones that turned from the dawn of thy
    day,
In the blaze of its noon shall but wither away.

In thy kingdom of love shall all violence cease,
Thine exactors be justice, thine officers peace,
Thy people all righteous, and truth all thy ways,
Thy walls called salvation, thine open gates praise.

Jehovah, thy beauty, thy brightness, thy crown,
Thy moon shall not wane, and thy sun ne'er go down,
And the tide of thy glory no ebbing to know,
Shall an ocean of light round the universe flow.

# "LET THERE BE LIGHT."

WRITTEN FOR THE LAYING OF THE CORNER-STONE
OF ST. PAUL'S COLLEGE, OCT. 15, 1836.

WHEN Earth's foundation stone was laid,
Let there be Light, Jehovah said;
Night from her chaos throne was hurled,
And morning blest the embryo world.

Let there be Light: again He spoke;
The storm of fire from Sinai broke;
Let there be Light: the Rainbow shone
In beauty round Messiah's throne.

Let there be Light: the light that streams
Rich from the Cross, in living beams,
Whence science gilds her fairest rays,
And genius burns with hallowed blaze.

Let there be Light: the potent word
That stirs to life where'er 'tis heard;
Utter it forth—Heaven's watchword still—
From vale to vale, from hill to hill.

Let there be Light : the high command
Be pledge and signal of our band :
Who vow to that akin we claim,
Fellows and friends, whate'er their name.

Let there be Light : our banner high
Shall catch the radiance of the sky,
Float on its breeze—triumphant—free—
Till God repeal His first decree.

# THE BLESSED NAME JESUS.

AN EVANGELICAL ROSARY.

Jesu's name shall ever be
For my heart, its Rosary;
I will tell it o'er and o'er,
Always dearer than before.

*Ave Mary*, may not be
For my heart its Rosary;
Jesus, Saviour, all in all—
Other name why should I call.

Morning hymns and evening lays,
Noontide prayer and midnight praise,
Heart and voice, and tune and time
Jesu's name they all shall chime.

Descant sweet, unceasing chant,
Other name my spirit can't—
Time bring what it may along,
Jesus still the unchanging song.

Redolent with healing balm,
Pleasure's charm and trouble's calm; ·
All of Heaven my hope and claim,
Grace on grace in Jesu's name.

In my soul each deepest chord
Ring it out, One Saviour Lord ;
Jesus, the eternal hymn
Forth from saint and seraphim.

Jesus, breathe my every breath—
Jesus, on my last in death—
Jesus, rest in paradise—
Jesus, glory in the skies !

1842.

# LINES

ON HEARING SOME GAY MUSIC OF MY BROTHER'S, SOON
AFTER HIS DECEASE.

THOSE blithesome notes ! ah me, how strange,
  They strike upon my ear !
The same he touched—and yet a change
  In every tone I hear.

So plaintive gay—at once they chime
  A sweet discordant tone ;
The ear, but not the heart, keeps time—
  The harmony has flown.

Like funeral bells in muffled gloom
  Pealing a merry air ;
Or brilliant flowers upon a tomb,
  Blooming so sadly fair.

Then play some hallowed strain he wrote,
  No tune of earthly leaven—
Something to mingle with the note
  I ween he chants in Heaven !

## "THY KINGDOM COME."

King of kings, and wilt Thou deign,
O'er this wayward heart to reign?
Other Sovereign, none I'll own;
Rule here, Lord, and rule alone.

Then, like heaven's angelic bands,
Waiting for Thine high commands,
All my powers shall wait on Thee,
Captive, yet divinely free.

At Thy word my Will shall bow,
Judgment, Reason, bending low,
Hope, Desire, and every thought,
Into glad obedience brought.

Zeal shall haste on eager wing,
Hourly some new gift to bring,
Wisdom, humbly casting down
At Thy feet her golden crown.

Tuned by Thee in sweet accord,
All shall sing their gracious Lord;

Love, the leader of the quire,
Breathing round her seraph fire.

Be it so—my heart's Thy throne;
All my powers Thy sceptre own,
And, with them on Thine own hill,
Live rejoicing in Thy will.

# LINES

You bid me dedicate your book,
   Denial is in vain,
Say, then, to whom my muse shall look
   To hear the votive strain.

To genius, surely, if her fire
   With truth were always bright,
If ne'er she strung a syren lyre
   Nor flashed a dazzling light.

To friendship, rather, if her heart
   Were always warm and pure,
And always with an angel's art
   To goodness would allure.

Nay, then, to virtue's patronage
   The volume I resign;
And like it be thy heart a page
   For many a holy line.

# A FABLE.

*(The Thought Borrowed.)*

" Huzza for a show !
  Gaze, mortals below,"
Sang a rocket just ready to rise ;
" Neighbor lamp, fare thee well,
  Burn on in thy cell,
While I go to light up the skies."


It whizzed and it flashed,
  As upward it dashed,
With a train of magnificent fire ;
  The lamp's feeble light,
  Scarce attracted the sight,
While all the gay streamer admire.


In the midst of the shout,
  Alas ! it is out,
Down tumbles the stick to the ground :
  " Already returned,"
  Quoth the lamp it had spurned,
That was still shining gently around.

So steady and bright,
Like the lamp's useful light,
Be the zeal I would cherish and prize ;
While the fierce rocket zeal,
That a madcap may feel,
Spouts fire a moment, and dies.

# A CHRISTMAS CAROL.

Made for the Boys of St. Paul's College—the Chorus adapted from one of the Rev. A. C. Coxe's Christian Ballads.

CAROL, brothers, carol;
  Carol joyfully;
Carol the good tidings,
  Carol merrilie—
And pray a gladsome Christmas
  For all good Christian men;
Carol, brothers, carol,
  Christmas times again.

Carol ye, with gladness
  Not in songs of earth;
On the Saviour's birth-day,
  Hallowed be our mirth;
While a thousand blessings
  Fill our hearts with glee;
Christmas-day we'll keep, the
  Feast of Charity!

4*

At the joyous table,
Think of those who've none—
The orphan and the widow,
Hungry and alone;
Bountiful your offerings,
To the altar bring;
Let the poor and needy
Christmas carols sing.

Listening angel music,
Discord sure must cease;
Who dare hate his brother,
On this day of peace?
While the heavens are telling
To mankind good-will,
Only love and kindness
Every bosom fill.

Let our hearts, responding
To the seraph band,
Wish this morning's sunshine
Bright in every land!
Word, and deed, and prayer,
Speed the grateful sound,
Bidding merry Christmas
All the world around.

1840.

# HYMN.

Jerusalem, Jerusalem,
 Name ever dear to me;
Oh, may at last my home be found,
 Jerusalem, in thee!

Oh, may these eyes thy crystal walls,
 And gates of pearl behold,
Thy jasper and thy sapphire stones,
 Thy streets of purest gold.

The alleluia of thy hymns
 Before the great I Am;
The harpers harping with their harps,
 The new song of the Lamb!

The white robes of thy ransomed hosts;
 The victor palms they bear;
Prophets, apostles, martyrs, saints,
 Dear friends, and kindred there.

No sun and moon with changing ray,
  To tell thy day and night;
The Lord Himself thy glory is,
  And Jesus is thy light.

Jerusalem, Jerusalem!
  Name ever dear to me ;
Oh, may at last my home be found,
  City of God, in thee !

# A CHRISTMAS CAROL.

[Written on the occasion of receiving a "Christmas Box" from
my former pupils of Flushing Institute and St. Paul's College,
in the form of a valuable and most interesting picture, which one
of them had learned I had much admired. The lines, as an
acknowledgment of their kindness, were recited to a number of
them who met in my church, for the purpose, on Christmas
morning—1856.]

"A MERRIE Christmas," merrie thrice,
    My friends, my children dear,
    More heartily that wish I've breathed
    Never, than to you here.

And now what shall my greeting be?
    What words shall I employ?
    I've tried—my heart won't go in prose,
    'Twill only sing its joy.

Seldom since ye were boys at school,
    I've penned a rhyming strain;
    The genius of your presence 'tis
    That wakes my muse again.

And ballads *are* for Christmas time;
  Then one I may essay,
On this which your kind hearts have made
  My happiest Christmas day.


For what delights a father more,
  Or what to him more dear,
Than when his sons in man's estate
  Unite his age to cheer?


I am no father—round my board
  Daughters nor sons will meet,
Like yours, that roused you at the dawn
  With Christmas kiss to greet.


Yet I can well endure the loss—
  I can, when such a band
Fain call their old schoolmaster Sire,
  And give their filial hand.


There's other parentage than that
  Which human ties accord—
May I not claim you without boast
  My children in the Lord?

'Twas all His ordering providence,
   His grace, I'll hope, as well,
That made my roof your boyhood's home,
   Still on your lives to tell.


Ye've sacred thoughts of that old home,
   Its chapel, prayers, and praise,
With songs and rites that made you love
   The church's festal days.


Those rites and songs—they've just gone by—
   That early Christmas scene :
At dawn had you been here you'd felt
   Like boys again, I ween.


*Hosanna, blessed He that comes,*
   Young choristers have sung :
*Magnificats* and *Glorias*
   Around the church have rung.


In shaking hands, as once we did,
   With voice and hearts in chime,
With Christmas gifts to feast the poor,
   We've had a right good time.

That Christmas gift of yours last eve—
Greater no child's delight,
With glistening eyes at *Santa Claus*,
Than mine was at the sight.


Thanks for a gift of costly price,
A noble work of art,
More precious for the argument
Its graphic forms impart.


Grand the idea that canvas shows:*
The open Word of God,
Enlightening, blessing, comforting
Souls freed from priestly rod.


* The painting—three feet by two—by Hübner, the first
artist of the Protestant branch of the Düsseldorf school, repre-
sents the interior of a German cottage with the rustic family
engaged with the Holy Scriptures. A boy reading from the
Bible forms the centre of the group. His grand-parents are
listening—the mother lighted up with joy in believing, the
father pondering what he hears with a more reasoning faith.
The sister of the boy, with half-absent looks, is patiently waiting,
with folded arms, until he is done, leaning on the back of the
chair which he occupies as the seat of honour, for the time, in
consideration of his office. In the foreground is apparently the

A youth the priest—a peasant's cot
　　The hallowed house of prayer—
No jewelled altar, yet full sweet
　　The incense rising there.


No mediator save the One
　　To man before his Lord:
He for himself the pardon reads,
　　The great High-Priest's own word.


That Gospel faith (to set it forth,
　　The artist's high design),
That faith your gift a pledge shall be,
　　For ever yours and mine.


And more, I trow, your present means:
　　That ye've rememberéd
How young and old, from first to last,
　　The Bible lesson said.


widowed mother of the children, who has returned with them to
the old home. She listens with the composure of calm reverence
and pious attention. Light through an opening in the roof seems
to hint at illumination from above. The details of the work are
admirable.

That Bible lesson—Oh, deem not
  For boyish days a rule,
But o'er and o'er, till got by heart,
  Task in the life-long school.


For scholars yet, alike we are,
  Of one school or the other:
That of the world, alas! so full,
  Or that of Christ our Brother.


Our Brother, yea, our Brother He,
  The LORD, to-day appears:
Bone of our bone, flesh of our flesh,
  Humanity He wears:


To found His blessed school on earth,
  His Church, the school of Heaven,
Master and Teacher, Guide and Friend,
  To be, Himself has given.


Learn ye of Him, lowly and meek,
  Yield to his kind control;
His easy yoke, His burden light,
  With rest unto your soul.

Learn ye of Him, ye busy ones
  Toiling earth's lore to gain,
Year in, year out, with vexing thought—
  Vexing how oft in vain.


Christ's scholars ye, be taught of Him
  How fretting care shall cease,
In ways of His all pleasantness,
  In paths of His all peace.


Whate'er the task, whate'er the rule,
  Whate'er the class or place,
'Tis but the training of His love,
  His discipline of grace.


His scholars—*they'll* have holidays!
  Those holidays to come,
When all whom He has taught shall meet,
  As brothers meet at home.


E'en now He makes a brother's feast,
  'Tis spread this blessed day—
We'll gather there—oh, why not all?
  Can any say Him, nay?

A brother's feast—the first-born He
  Amid that Brotherhood,
Of all in every age and clime
  Who true to him have stood.


In East or West, in North or South,
  Their Table is but one,
And theirs the only fellowship
  Never to end begun.


Never to end—yea, ever new,
  In bright perennial youth,
There in the Father's house—the Home
  Of perfect Love, and Truth.


Christ bring ye thither, my dear sons,
  This be my Christmas prayer—
This benison my heart's desire :
  *All here be numbered there !*


Amen, I know, your hearts reply,—
  Then pledge the vow with me :
Henceforth we'll live, that we may keep,
  Christmas eternally

And now all glory, honour, praise
To God, the Incarnate Son,
The Father, and the Holy Ghost,
For ever Three in One.

5*

# HYMN AT SEA.

FOR THE MISSIONARIES TO CHINA, JULY, 1859.

COME, Brothers, as we voyage along,
To Him we love lift up the song,
Who first loved us, His own delight,
Bless day by day, bless night by night.

Jesus, we sing, where'er we are,
On native shores, or borne afar ;
The same sweet well-spring of the soul,
Exhaustless as these waters roll.

Jesus, the Name o'er every name,
Of light and love the eternal flame ;
With that aglow be all our ways,
Thought, word, and deed, one psalm of praise.

Thy missioners, thus, oh, Christ, we'll be,
Nothing ourselves—all, all of Thee ;
Only Thy strength be seen in ours,
Thy might alone our mightiest powers.

Then, while we ask the favouring gale,
Still more we pray ; Thy breath prevail,
Creating prophets of Thy word,
Souls to subdue to Thee their Lord—

Lifting their voice with trumpet calls,
Till, as the last Pagoda falls,
O'er Buddha's realms the anthem rings,
Christ, Lord of Lords, and King of Kings.

Amen, amen, so let it be,
All praise to Thee, Thou One in Three,
New honour, glory, power be given
By hosts on earth with hosts in Heaven.

# "COME FOLLOW ME."

WRITTEN FOR THE RECEPTION OF A "SISTER" AT ST. LUKE'S HOSPITAL.

THINE Handmaid, Saviour! can it be?
Such honour dost Thou put on me?
To wait on Thee—do Thy commands—
The works once hallowed by Thy hands?

Daily thy mercy paths to go,
Bearing Thy balm for every woe,
Thy sick and weary ones to cheer,
Bid them Thy words of pity hear—

Parting with earth Thy cross to bear,
Content thy poverty to share,
Rich in Thy Love—Thou blessed Lord,
This life to me dost Thou accord?

Oh marvellous grace—yea even so!
The call I heard—'twas thine I know—
" Come follow me ;" the Heavenly voice,
How could it but constrain my choice!

My heart's free choice, yet bound by Thee;
Thrice welcome, sweet captivity,
My soul and all its powers to fill
With love of Thee and Thy dear will.

Lord, give but light to show the way,
Strength from Thyself to be my stay,
Grace, always, grace to feel Thee nigh—
Thine Handmaid then, I live and die.

1859.

# GOOD BYE.

Written for the Infant School of the Church of the Ascension, New York, on Parting with their Pastor to become Assistant Bishop of Ohio.

OFT in song our voices ringing,
  Thou hast heard and joined our cry,
Now no strain of gladness bringing
  We have come to sing good bye.
          Dearest Pastor,
  We have come to sing good bye.

Thanks for all thy faithful teaching,
  Patient with our heedless years ;
Thanks for thy sweet stories, preaching
  Jesus to our infant ears.
          Dearest Pastor,
  Thanks on thanks with our good bye.

Every Lord's day shall remind us
  Of thy loving presence here,
And long years in age still find us
  Clinging to thy memory dear.
          Dearest Pastor,
  Ever in our hearts, good bye.

God be with thee, friend and father,
    Doing well the shepherd's part;
Seeking still the lambs to gather,
    Bearing them anear thy heart.
              Dearest Pastor,
Happy they thy flock, good bye.

Parting—parted not in Jesus,
    That great Shepherd of the sheep,
Ransomed by his blood most precious,
    Thee and us will ever keep.
              Dearest Pastor,
With this prayer, our last good bye.

1859.

# A LETTER PATERNAL.

\*      \*      \*      \*      \*

MAN may make Bishops, Christ alone
Makes those whom He vouchsafes to own,
Sprung of pure apostolic race,
The sure succession of His grace.

Then may His unction *you* anoint;
His hands imposing *you* appoint,
Rich in the gifts which they impart,
True Bishops after His own heart.

His blood-bought flock your charge to keep,
Forth in green pastures lead the sheep,
Carry the lambs, the weak upbear,
The meanest not beneath your care.

Nor them alone within the fold,
The wanderers far around behold;
Bring in the outcast, lame, and blind,
The lost ones on the mountains find.

Faithful dispense the Master's word,
Let no uncertain sounds be heard ;
Christ's gospellers, all rightly tell
His saving grace from sin and hell.


The Church needs Bishops who can preach,
As well as rule their flocks and teach,
Men ever first and foremost found,
In trumpet tones the truth to sound.


Who should be such but they who call
Their office one with that of Paul ;
Like Paul then preach, nor aught beside
Christ Jesus, and Him crucified.


Apostles still may God inspire,
Touched with the old supernal fire,
Bold His whole counsel to proclaim ;
Their power, the One Almighty Name.


The Lord has such—nor only where
Ye fain would see them—then beware
Lest, as ye coldly from them turn,
His own anointed ones ye spurn.

What He hath wrought, ye'd not reverse—
Whom He hath blessed, ye would not curse—
Nay, give to all the brother's hand,
Who keep with you His last command.


On them, on you, oh, be outpoured
The seven-fold Spirit of the Lord,
Making your heart strong, and rejoice
To lift anew, for God, your voice.


As watchmen on the tower set high,
Be silent day nor night your cry;
For Zion's sake hold not your peace,
For dear Jerusalem never cease.


So wear your lawn—no robe of state—
A prophet's robe—in that be great;
Your crozier bear, but not to wage,
Lording it o'er God's heritage.


Nor that in you, my sons, I fear—
Too well approved your long career,
As Christian pastors—yet have care
In using power, the churchman's snare.

Your power be love, and only love,
Proving your office from above,
While young and old, like children all,
You, Sires in God, delight to call.

When the Chief Shepherd shall appear,
Gathering his consecrated near,
Your mitre then, so worn below,
A crown upon your brow shall glow.

How shall it be? by prayer, by prayer—
Prayer, instant, always, everywhere—
For strengthening in the inner man,
With might of Him whose Spirit can.

Work in you both to do and will;
Make you his pleasure to fulfil;
Created in His Son, to stand,
The workmanship of His own hand.

So be complete your consecration,
In your eternal coronation!

1859.

# LINES

TO A DEAR FRIEND, RECENTLY DEPRIVED OF HER
SIGHT.

THE violet flowers, the meadows green,
The concave blue, the golden sun,
The face of friends, their winsome mien,
All, all, to thee, for ever done.

And yet no murmuring at thy lot;
No weary discontent I hear;
Nay, God, thy God, withholdeth not
His own sweet light within to cheer.

Serene, I see it in thy face,
E'en as if not of sight bereft,
Telling of calm submissive grace,
Wise to enjoy what still is left.

Music there's left, whose notes ne'er tire,
Home's harmonies, to fill thine ear;
The descant of the hearth-stone choir,
The tones of love in voices dear.

Thanks only hast thou for the Lord,
  Granting such answer to thy prayers :
Daughters and sons who fear His word,
  And joy to make thy wishes theirs.


Wealth, too, brings many a gladsome mood,
  Since twice with that endowed thou art;
Rich in the means of doing good,
  Yet richer in the generous heart.


The hungry whom thy bounty feeds,
  The cold and naked by thee clad,
The widow gladdened in her weeds,
  The fatherless no longer sad—


The sick ones in their hallowed ward,
  With nursing sisters at their side,
Schools of the prophets of the Lord,
  Never in want by thee denied—


Such mercies while thy liberal mind
  Rejoices still to multiply,
To fairest scenes thou art not blind,
  No darkness in thy spirit's eye.
6*

And more and more of inward sight,
    May God vouchsafe thee, dearest friend ;
Illume thee for the realms of light,
    Thine eyes immortal vision lend—


His glorious dwelling to behold !
    His beautiful Jerusalem !
Its pearl, and emerald, and gold,
    Its twelve foundations, each a gem.


That city's light, Jehovah's face,
    The Lamb once slain, the mid-day sun ;
Before the throne, there crowned by grace,
    Be thou and thine, in Christ made one !

1859.

*"Who keep with you His last command."*

That is, Christ's parting command to His Apostles, to "Go preach the Gospel to every creature." The sentiment implied in the ninth and tenth verses of the "Letter Paternal," is, that Bishops acting on that command, in virtue of their historic succession from the Apostles, should recognise all who fulfil the great object of the command, whether they be in the line of such succession or not. If this is not High Church doctrine, neither is it low. The Episcopal Church will take a more elevated stand as a witness for her Lord, when, instead of indiscriminately ignoring all preachers beyond her pale, she distinguishes those who hold "the truth as it is in Jesus," and gives some sign of fellowship with them as co-workers in proclaiming the Gospel. Thus to discern and welcome the Faith wherever found, would manifest a pure affection for it, and would be an office worthy of a church, the acknowledged centre of Protestant Christendom.